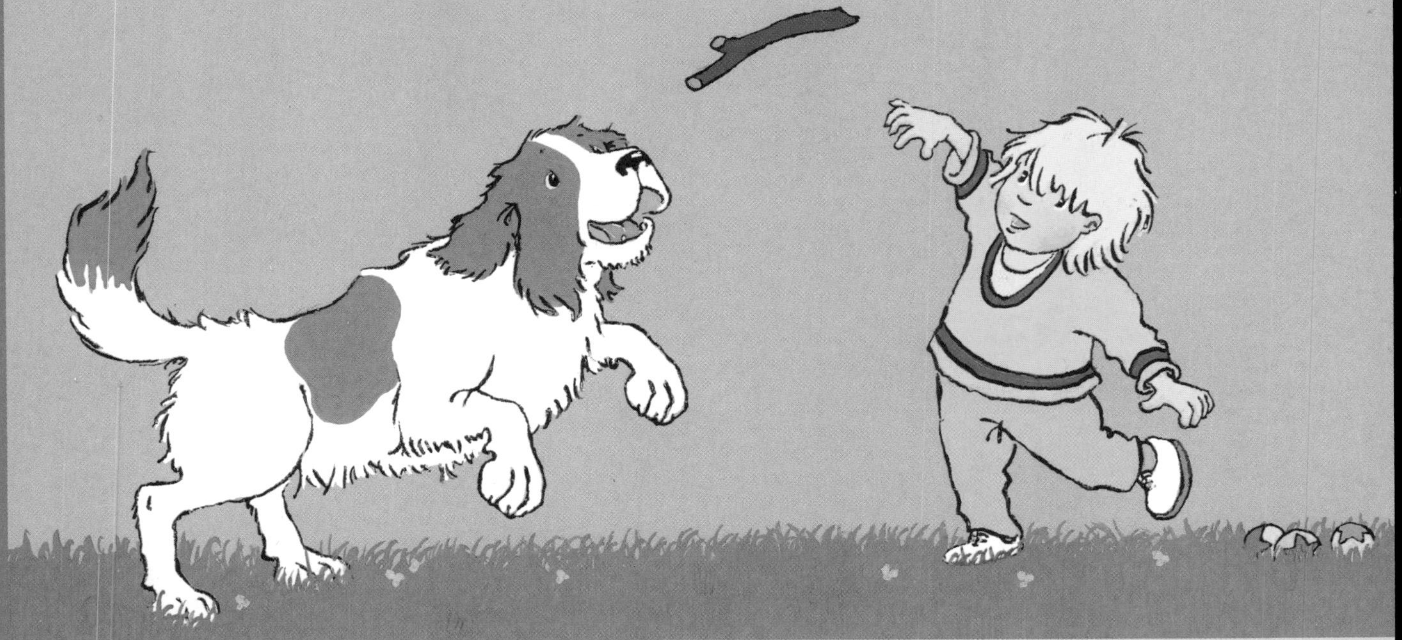

Winnie and Annie play catch.

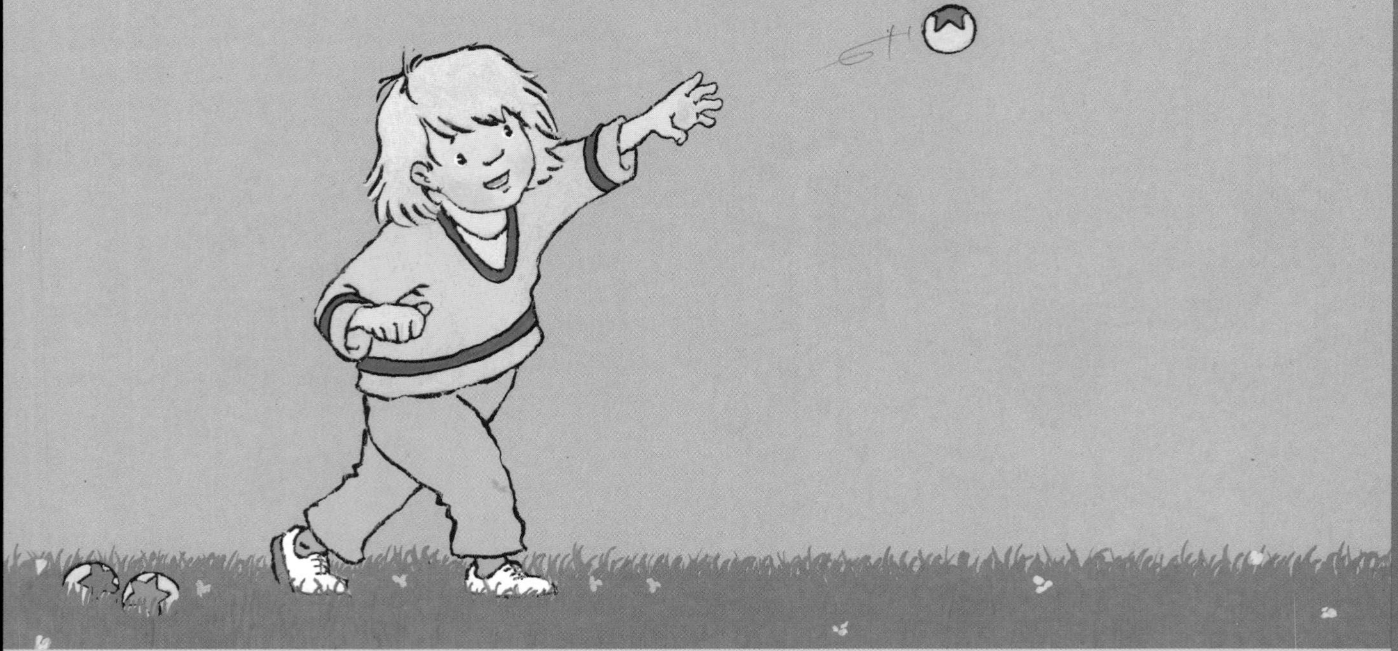

Annie throws a ball.

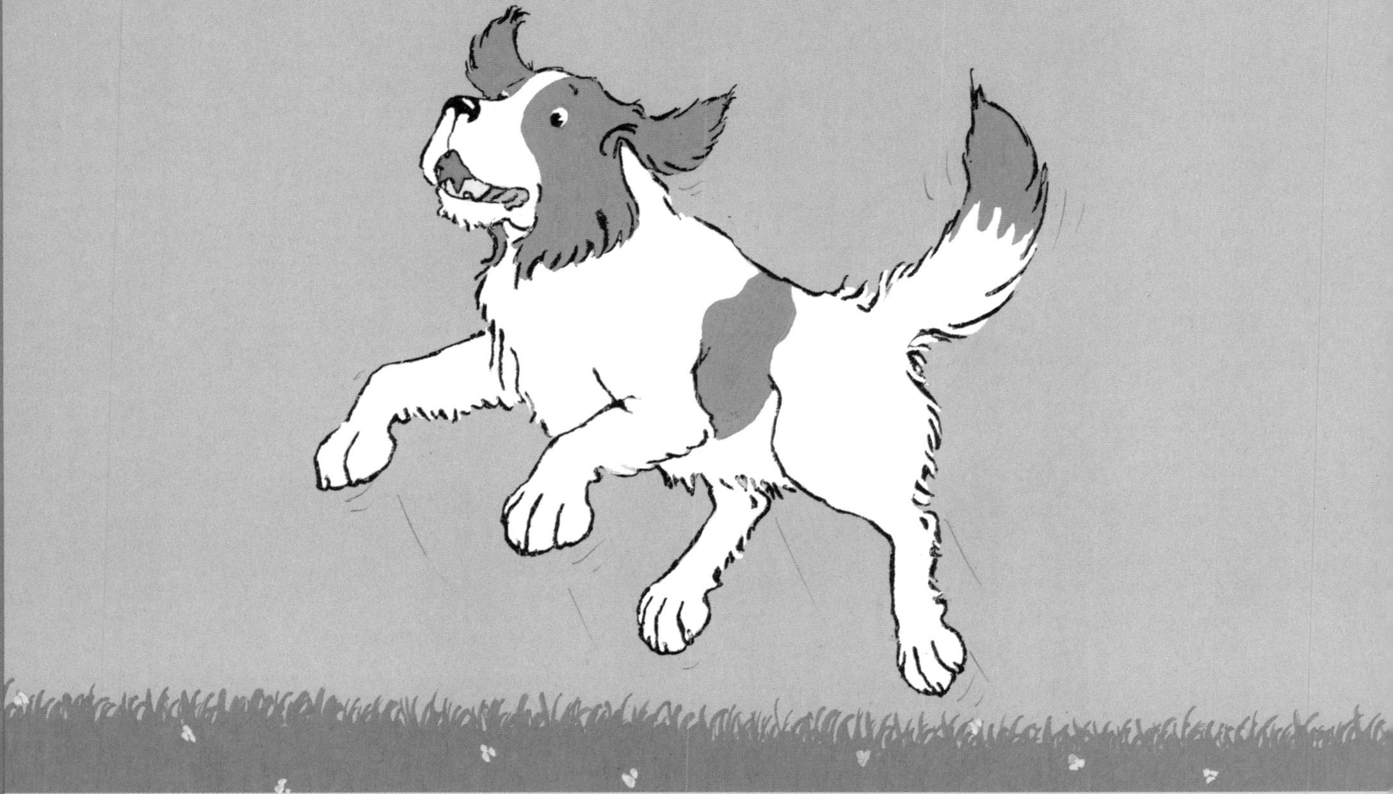

Winnie catches it.

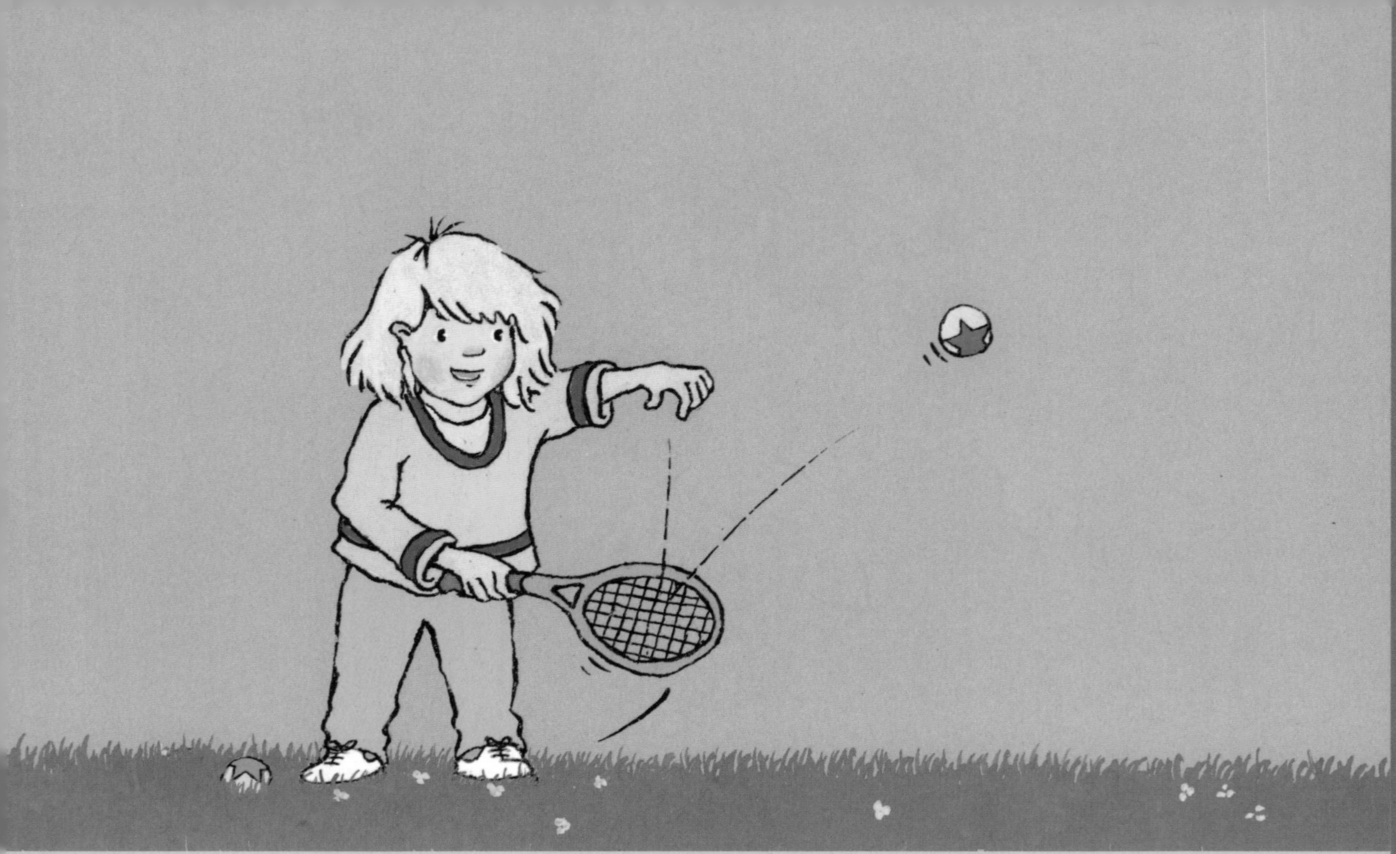

Annie hits a ball.

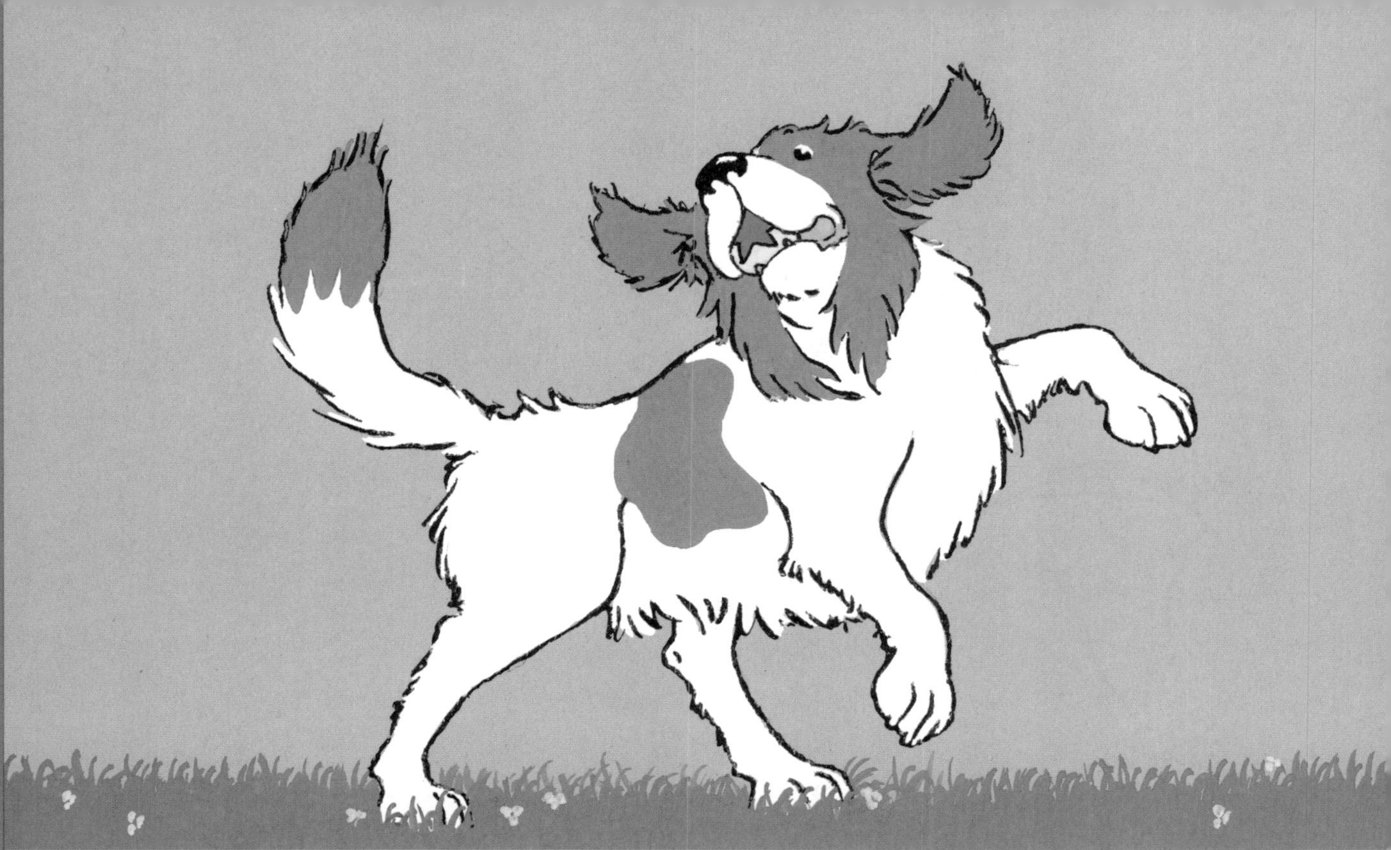

Winnie catches it.

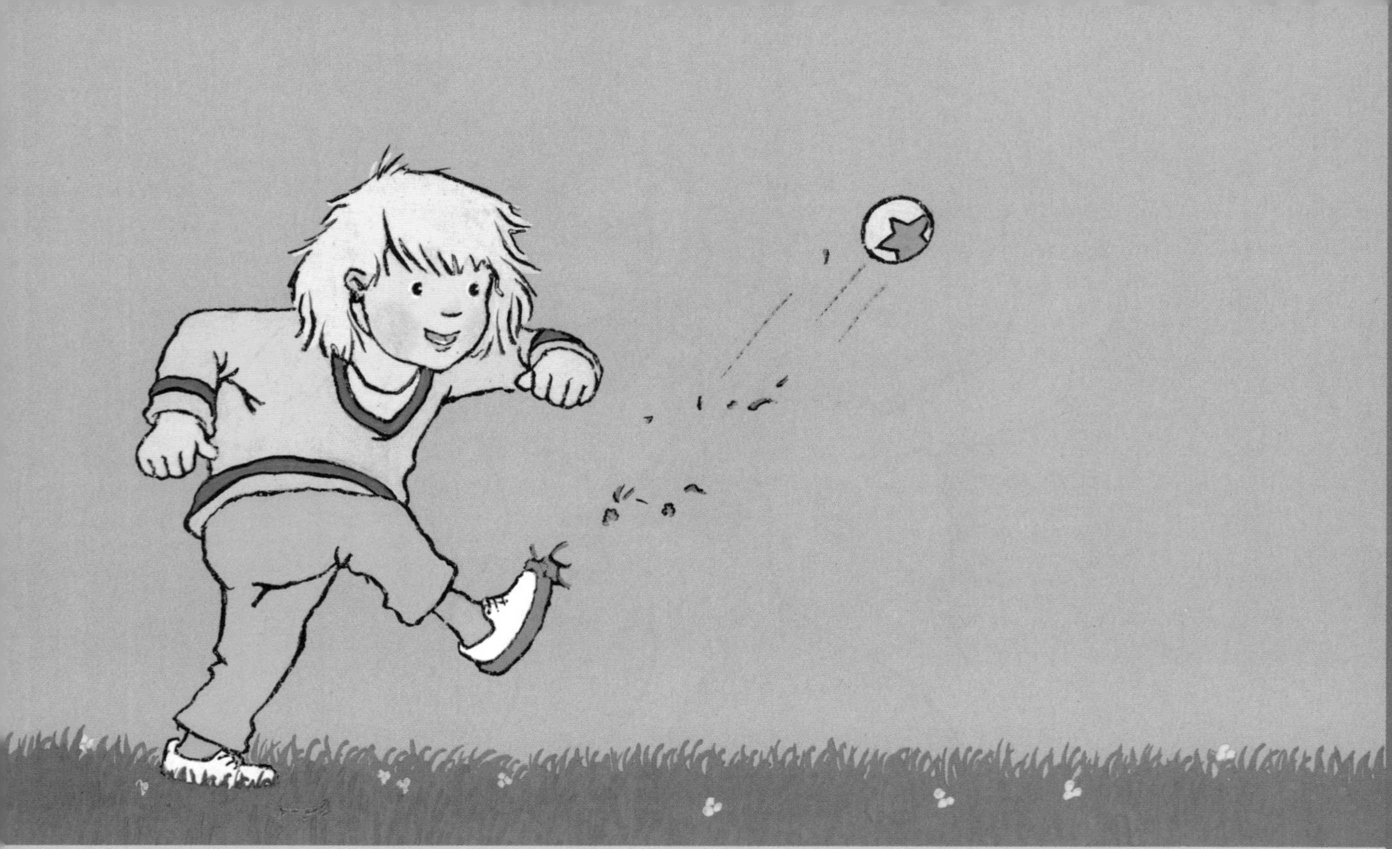

Annie kicks a ball.

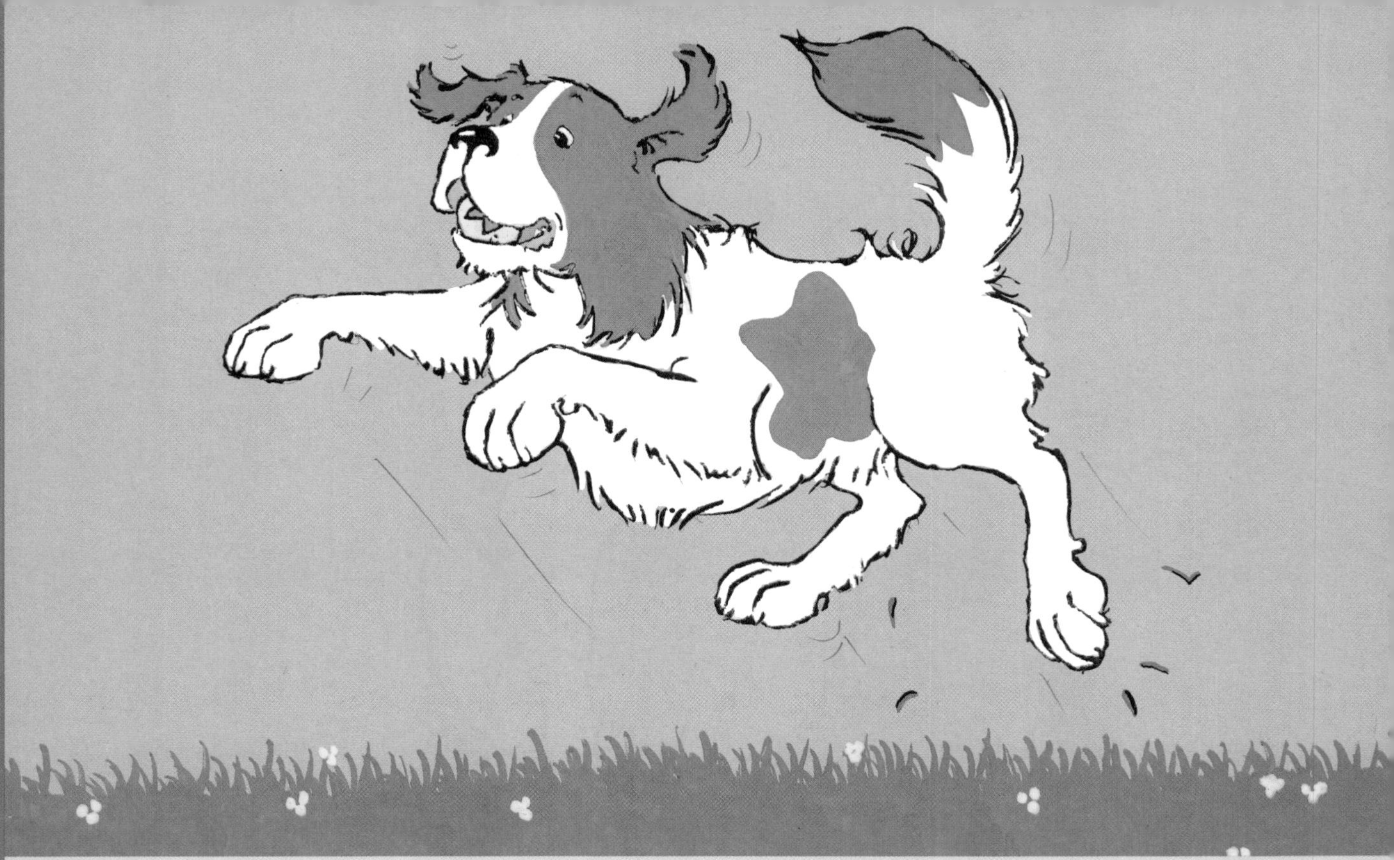

Winnie catches it.

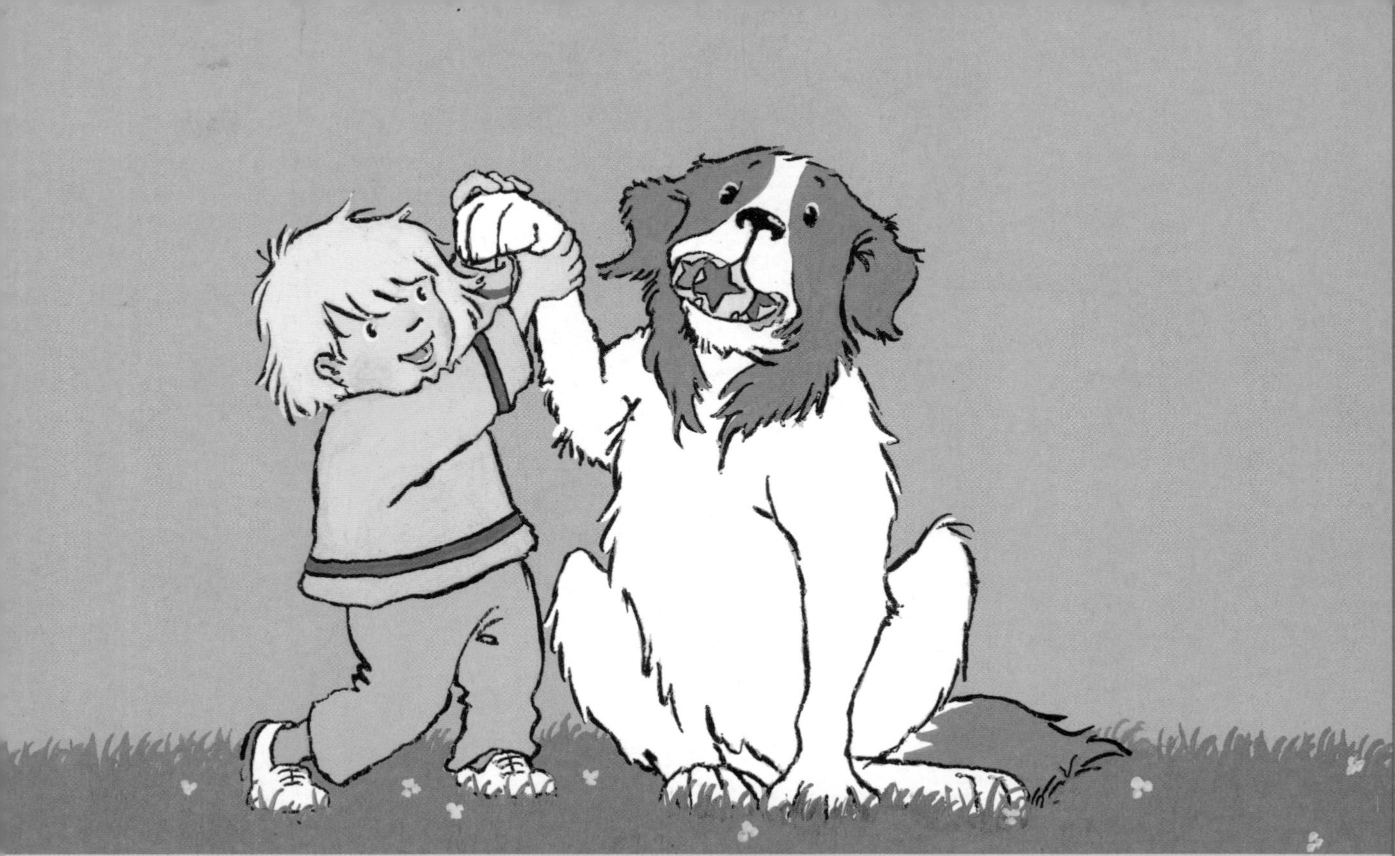

Winnie wins the game.